Fibber E. Frog

By Al Newman
Illustrated by Jim Doody

Publisher's Cataloging in Publication
(Prepared by Quality Books Inc.)

Newman, Alfred T.
    Fibber E. Frog / by Al Newman; illustrated by Jim Doody.
    p. cm.
    Audience: Ages 3 through 9
    SUMMARY: Fibber E. Frog is a frog who tells fibs and lies to cover up for his own insecurity. Readers can help him learn to be himself.
    Preassigned LCCN: 93-77685.
    ISBN 0-89334-213-0 (hard.)
    ISBN 0-89334-217-3 (pbk.)

    1. Frogs—Juvenile fiction. 2. Truthfulness and falsehood—Juvenile fiction. 3. Frogs—Fiction. 4. Honesty—Fiction. I. Doody, James J., ill. II. Title.

PZ7 .N4953F53 1993   [E]
                                      QBI93-552

Humanics Children's House
P.O. Box 7400
Atlanta, GA 30357
Humanics Children's House is an imprint of Humanics Limited.
Copyright © 1993 Humanics Limited.
All rights reserved.
Printed in the United States of America.
10 9 8 7 6 5 4 3 2 1

Fibber E. Frog isn't famous or rich.

He's just a poor frog

who lives in a ditch.

NOW PLAYING

FIBBER E. FROG

AND THE POLLYWOGS

All day long
he sits on a log,
telling stories
to pollywogs.

Some stories are true,
but some are not . . .

. . . because Fibber E. Frog fibs a lot!

Fibbit, fibbit, fibbit
he croaks.

And in between fibs,
he tells a few jokes.

Now why would a frog
like Fibber E. lie?

Is he just a born fibber?

A really bad guy?

The simple truth
is rather sad.
Because Fibber E. Frog
doesn't mean to be bad . . .

. . . he just doesn't think
he's important enough!

So he makes up stories

that are nothing but fluff!

This frog needs your help!

You can help set him straight.

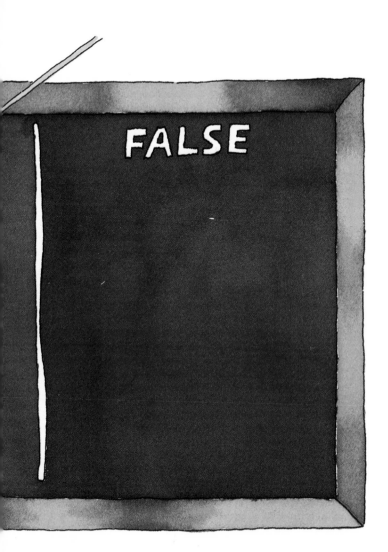

Tell him to just be himself.

He doesn't have to be great!

People will like him if he's honest and fair.

But no one likes frogs
who are full of hot air!

Help Fibber E. Frog
learn not to say Fibbit.

Everyone knows a frog
should say Ribbit!

50,926

DATE DUE

Ag 30 '94	Ag 7		
Se 6 '94	Ag 20 '97		
So 13 '94	28		
Se 15 '94	Sa		
Se 21 '94	A 13 0 0		
Nov 1 '94	Aug 23		
Se 7 '95	DEC 0 3 2007		
Apr 4 96	APR 1-2 2018		
May 22 96	APR 0 4 2014		
Jul 22 95			
Jun 5 '97			
Jul 9 '97			

E
New   Newman, Al
             Fibber E. Frog